DESCENDANTS
Wicked World

based on the animated shorts
written by Julia Miranda

studio fun

A READER'S DIGEST COMPANY

White Plains, New York • Montréal, Québec • Bath, United Kingdom

I t's time for the Heroes and Heroines Festival in Auradon, and Evie has made cupcakes to compete with the ones Audrey made last year. She runs into the Do-It-Your-Selfie tent to find Mal.

Last year, Audrey's cupcakes were like an explosion of deliciousness.

You have to help me!

What's the emergency?

This!

Evie shows Mal the plate she is carrying.

Evie admits that she volunteered to make cupcakes for the carnival—but she can't bake. She combined all the elements of the periodic table into the batch, and now she needs Mal's help.

Use your magic!

No way!

"I'm trying to be good, remember?" replies Mal.

"Magic for a good cause is automatically good!" Evie declares.

"I don't think it really works that way," Mal argues. But Evie begs Mal to help her, and Mal finally agrees—just this once.

Please, please, please!

There are 118 elements in the periodic table.

On the Isle of the Lost, evil minion bakers made all the cupcakes!

Consulting her spell book, Mal begins.

"Oh, Magic Spell Book . . ."

Evie bites into one of the cupcakes. "Make no haste and turn Evie's cupcakes . . . into an explosion . . . of—"

EW!

BAM!

"You didn't let me finish the spell!" Mal cries. "Instead of an explosion of taste, we made an explosion of . . . cupcakes!"

Evie included sulfur in her cupcake recipe—causing an explosive chemical reaction!

EVIE AND MAL: SWEET FRIENDS OR SWEET FIENDS??

5

2 MAL'S DIGI-IMAGE PROBLEM

Ben finds Mal in the Do-It-Your-Selfie tent.

"Hey, Mal, busy?"

Yeah, I'm in the zone.

Ben asks if she can de-zone.

"Not a word, but I'll forgive you 'cause you're cute . . . but not cute enough to make me lose my focus . . . there's been a bit of an 'incident.'"

"Oh yeah, your digi-image."

"That's definitely not a word," she says.

"Your digital image. Digi-image," Ben explains.

"Still not a word," Mal insists.

Ben looks at his phone and shows her the negative posts.

This!

Mal reads.

"That's trending by the way," Ben observes.

Mal's a princess in waiting, alright... a princess in waiting to mess up! Princess-aster.

#Princess-aster

"Okay, my people may be evil, but what you Auradon kids are doing to the English language is cruel. Not to worry . . . I'll make it up to Audrey by posting this wicked portrait of her as her favorite heroine!" Mal reveals a spray-painted portrait of Audrey in Sleeping Beauty's dress.

Flora and Merryweather fought over the color of Sleeping Beauty's gown—pink prevailed over blue.

Ben is surprised. "Her mom! So, Maleficient's daughter painting Sleeping Beauty's daughter, as Sleeping Beauty, is supposed to help your digi-image?"

Do you remember Family Day?

Mal shudders. *"Family Day.* So, what, I should do some un-Sleeping Beautying?"

Ben smiles. "That's not a word."

"I'm learning how to be Auradonian," Mal says. "C'mon, it's not like I gave her Captain Hook's coat!" Then, kidding around, she intones:

Captain Hook is the pirate captain of the brig *Jolly Roger.*

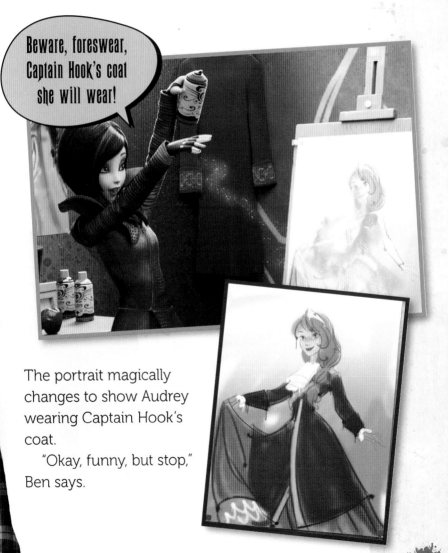

Beware, foreswear, Captain Hook's coat she will wear!

The portrait magically changes to show Audrey wearing Captain Hook's coat.

"Okay, funny, but stop," Ben says.

Mal continues, "Beware, foreswear, Cruella's stole might give a scare!" Cruella's stole appears on Audrey's portrait.

Cruella's stole is made of faux Dalmatian fur!

Mal, enough with the magic!

"Beware, foreswear, sprout my mother's horns from Audrey's hair!"

Ben warns, "Okay, but change it back before someone—"

An arms pops into the tent and takes a photo of the portrait.

"—sees it," Ben finishes his thought.

Mal looks at her phone.

SOZ, LOOKS LIKE WE HAVE R ANSWER ABOUT MAL...MAYBE SHE'S NOT SO "GOOD" AFTER ALL. SMH

"I . . . have a digi-image problem."

"**N**o! Gross! No!" A frustrated Audrey flips through the clothes hanging in her closet, pointing out the offending articles, as Jane looks on. Audrey pulls out a dress, then tosses it toward Jane.

That one looks nice.

The actual saying is, "Magic Mirror on the wall, who is the fairest one of all?"

"Nice?! The saying isn't 'Mirror, mirror, on the wall, who's the nicest of them all?'" Audrey snipes.

"I dunno, Audrey," Jane says. I kinda had to learn the hard way that it's not all about what you look like—"

"Ugh, everybody's so into their edgy VK style and dark-colored everything!"

"I don't think that they're so into their dark-colored everything. They're so into their—"

"Their hair! Duhzies! When Mal changed your hair, you went from 'Plain Jane' to 'Kinda Plain Jane,'" Audrey notes.

Magic me!

But Jane tells her, "I don't have magic."

Audrey disagrees. She thinks Fairy Godmother and Maleficent are the most powerful people ever.

"I never really thought about it that way . . . "
Jane realizes.

Audrey asks Jane about the spell Mal did for
everyone's hair.

"For me, she said 'new hair,' but for Lonnie,
she said 'cool hair,'" Jane muses.

Audrey says, "I'll take both." She sits down in
front of Jane. "Go ahead."

Jane hesitates. "I don't know, I—"

"I really appreciate this. You're a true friend, Jane," Audrey tells her.

Being told she's a true friend hits Jane's Achilles heel—now she has to help Audrey and starts to recite the spell. Audrey closes her eyes and smiles. She can't wait for her new do.

"Beware, foreswear, replace the old with . . . something really out there?"

Suddenly, a poof of smoke blows up around Audrey's head. When the dust settles, Audrey's new hair is a hot mess. Jane is horrified.

But Audrey is excited. "Do I look different?"

"Definitely," Jane confirms.

"Yes!" Audrey exclaims. She takes a picture with her phone. "Post it!"

al is trying to fix her portrait of Belle and Beast in the Do-It-Yourselfie booth, when a distraught Audrey bursts in, shaking her phone angrily. Audrey still has the crazy hairstyle. Jane follows, close behind.

Hi. Can I help you?

This selfie is ruining my life!

Mal gasps.

I mean . . . that looks great!

"If by great, you mean awful, then yes, it's great." Audrey's cell vibrates. "Fantastic, another comment." Audrey looks at her phone and screams.

WHO WORE IT BEST?

"I'm so sorry!" Jane apologizes. "I didn't even know I could do magic!" Then she gasps, "I can do magic!"

"Yup," Audrey confirms.

Still processing the revelation, Jane says, "I can do magic."

You can do magic?

"I gotta go lie down." Jane walks off in a daze. Then, Evie rushes in.

Everyone is talking about my cupcake disaster.

"Look at this post! 'Pastry chef? More like pastry death!' I don't think that's a compliment here."

Jay rushes in with a lamp.

Mal is exasperated. "Um, does anyone know how to knock?"

You're in a tent.

Jay thrusts the lamp into Mal's hands. "Hold onto this for me. It's very important." Before rushing off, he notices Audrey. "Nice hair."

"Really?" Audrey asks, hopefully.

"No. But I'm trying to learn how to be nice," Jay says, before leaving the tent.

Audrey turns and grabs Mal. "You have to fix my hair!"

Evie insists Mal has to help her first.

Jordan rushes in and sees Mal holding her lamp.

Thief! You stole my lamp!

"What? No," Mal defends herself.

"Cool it, Jordan," Audrey says. "Mal will help you when she's done with me."

"I think you mean, when she's done with me," corrects Evie.

"Did you get paint on my lamp?!" Jordan is not happy.

Mal looks down and, sure enough, there is some paint on the lamp. She begins rubbing off the paint.

"You're ruining my lamp!" yells Jordan, who grabs the lamp and leaves.

Completely overwhelmed by the chaos, Mal thinks aloud to herself, "Ugh, stuff like this never happened on the Isle of the Lost."

Then Ben enters the booth.

Carlos rushes into the booth. "Hey guys! Jay got me a new phone!" He looks around, but no one is there.

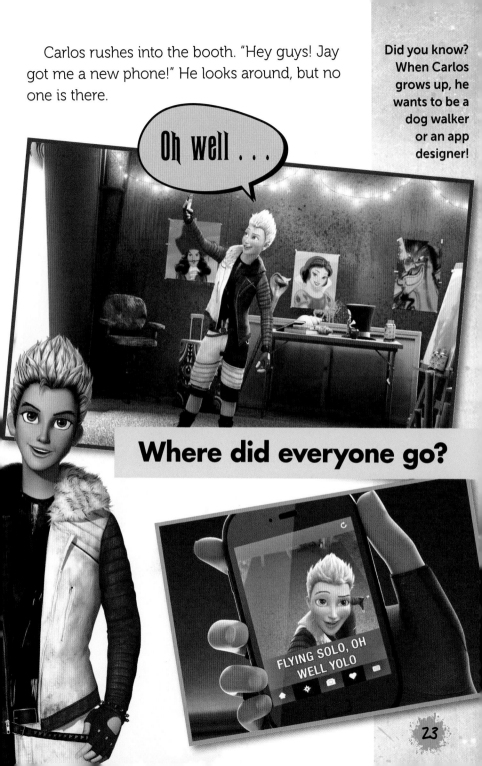

Oh well . . .

Where did everyone go?

FLYING SOLO, OH WELL YOLO

With a poof of smoke, Mal, Evie, Audrey, and Ben are magically transported to the Isle of the Lost. Ben and Audrey look around at the gritty surroundings, stunned.

Audrey's crazy hairdo is transformed back to normal after they are magically transported to the Isle of the Lost.

"We're on the Isle of the Lost?!" Audrey screams. *"Ew! Ben! Save me!!"*

"Now I know why they say be careful what you wish for," comments Mal.

Holding onto Ben's arm, Audrey asks,

Does it say where we are?

Thanks to my dad, there's no service on the Isle of the Lost.

There is no wi-fi on the Isle of the Lost.

"So we can't find a way out of here?! Can we even selfie?" Audrey grabs Ben's phone. She snaps a quick selfie and then looks at it. "Okay, this place needs so many filters."

Suddenly, a street urchin runs between Ben and Audrey, knocking Ben down and dropping something on the ground.

"Oh, excuse me. Sorry," Ben says. "You dropped . . . my wallet."

Pickpockets are rampant on the Isle of the Lost.

"We should find a place to hide," Evie suggests.

"Uh, yeah, before anybody sees we're here!" Mal confirms. She spots a back door to a voodoo shop.

Moments later, the gang is inside the store— a treasure trove of voodoo oddities and bizarre tchotchkes.

Mal gravitates to a pile of books and picks one up: "*Dictatorship for Beginners.*"

On the other side of the store, Audrey notices a dress that she likes.

"Figures the only remotely interesting item here would be on the 'Must Go' rack."

The voodoo shop has two sets of Maleficent horns in stock. One is displayed on a shelf, the other on top of a cupboard, next to a top hat. Can you spot them?

Freddie is the daughter of Dr. Facilier, an evil bokor, or Voodoo witch doctor.

Are you stealing that?

I would never steal!

No, are you stealing that, when you could be stealing this?

Freddie was born on the Isle of the Lost.

Busted? Or to be trusted?

But Audrey is mortified.

"That's the whole point! It's what we do here," encourages Freddie.

Ben, Evie, and Mal walk over.

"Oh no," Evie says.

"Oh no, what?" Ben wants to know.

Mal explains, "It's Freddie."

"Freddie? Short for Frederique?" asks Ben.

"Short for 'Let's blow this voodoo stand,'" concludes Mal.

I n the voodoo shop, Freddie paces around Audrey and Ben like a lioness stalking prey. "Well, well, well! The famous Auradonian kids."

Freddie's small hat is called a fascinator.

Okay, Freddie, retract your claws.

But I just had them sharpened.

She's joking . . . I think.

Only two television channels are available on the Isle of the Lost: the Auradon News Network, featuring *Auradon Buzz* and *King Beast's Fireside Chats*, and Dungeon Shopping Network, featuring *Dungeon Deals*.

Freddie says, "Ahhh, look at these two. They're adorable." Ben and Audrey smile. "It's sickening," Freddie continues.

"And what, pray tell, are you going to do about it?" Freddie asks.

"Thought so," says Freddie.
"When I throw a party, I—I won't invite you!" threatens Audrey.
Freddie laughs in her face.

Then Evie says to Mal, "We really need to teach them how to smack talk."

"Do you remember the 'your mama' battles we used to have?" Mal asks.

A wall next to the shop door features Mal's graffiti art of her mother.

Yo mama so weak, old ladies help her across the street!

Yo mama so weak, instead of poison apples, she makes apple pie!

Yo mama so soft, the only spells she casts are cryin' spells!

Yo mama so soft, cats share pictures of her!

Oh, snap!

"Yo mama's so soft, she's . . . like . . . a pillow!" Audrey chimes in.

"Well, what do you know! These guys are even more lame than I imagined." Freddie laughs.

Okay, we may not frown and wear black, but we are **NOT** lame.

"We can be rotten, just like you guys," Audrey continues.

"Yeah!" Ben agrees. But then he says to Audrey, "We can?" She shoots him a look.

Uh, yeah. Check this out!

"I'd be happy to pay for damages," says Ben.
Audrey asks, "Are we going to jail?"

Freddie motions and whispers to a
mysterious person entering the store.

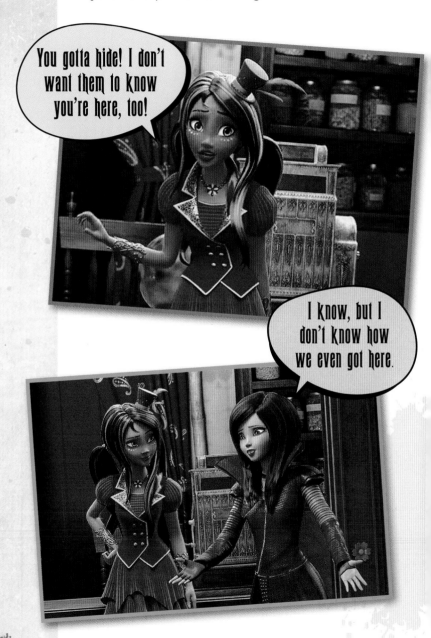

You gotta hide! I don't
want them to know
you're here, too!

I know, but I
don't know how
we even got here.

Mal continues, "I mean, one minute I was rubbing paint off Jordan's lamp, and then next— that's it! The lamp! I just wish we could ask her how we—"

Inside her lamp, Jordan is making a video for her AuraTube channel, showing how to make a proper pitcher of lemonade.

Suddenly, Mal, Evie, Ben, Audrey, and Freddie appear in a cloud of smoke, and Jordan screams.

Jordan hosts her own successful weekly Web show.

JORDAN HAS LEMONADE MELTDOWN

Jordan is the Genie of Agrabah's daughter.

Jordan is furious that Mal, Evie, Ben, Audrey, and Freddie have suddenly appeared inside her lamp.

> Excuse me, who drops into someone's lamp unannounced?!

> Sorry, I didn't even know you could drop into someone's lamp.

Visitors to Jordan's lamp are resized to fit within the space.

You can't be here dressed like that!

Jordan's lamp is a complete apartment and serves as her dorm room at Auradon Prep!

"Your lamp has a dress code?" Mal asks.

Jordan is incredulous. "Of course! I don't live in a jar! Ben, I'll spare you. No dude's been able to rock the harem pants since . . . well, my dad."

Ben is amused. "Thanks?"

Jordan snaps her fingers, and all the girls are suddenly dressed in genie-chic attire.

Blues and yellows make up Ben's signature style.

"Cute! Except if it were me I'd probably add a little more bling here . . . a little more sparkle over there," Evie says about her outfit.

"No? That's cool, I'm good!" Evie responds.
Mal can't believe the outfit she is wearing.

Chiffon is a lightweight, almost transparent fabric.

A sneeze is heard behind a curtain.

What was that?

ACHOO!

Freddie is quick to cover.

Uh, I sneezed. Uh . . . I'm allergic to lamps. It's hereditary.

Yeah, I have allergies, too. Get it from my dad.

Voodoo is a practice that uses charms and amulets to protect or harm others.

Freddie adds, "I get dolls from my dad."
Ben says, "Aw, that's—"
Freddie cuts him off. "Voodoo curse dolls."
Ben finishes his thought, "—terrifying."

Freddie continues. "He's so obsessed with ghosts that he knows all of their death-days, but he can never remember my birthday."

"Oh, man, my dad loves birthdays . . . he even made up this funny birthday dance . . . I wish you could see it." Ben says.

"I'm sure there's no room for another abominable villain in your beloved Auradon. I'll just have to envision your father's birthday promenade in my dreams," says Freddie.

Mal makes a gag motion, and Freddie smirks and then winks at her.

"Can we do this later? Like maybe not around me. And maybe not in my house?" Jordan asks.

"Okay . . . how do we get out of here?" Mal asks.

"Same way you got in. Wish your way out. Wish number three? Bye-eeee!" Jordan offers.

I'm telling you to go.

Mal is about to make a wish, but Evie stops her. "You really want to waste your last wish on getting out?"

"If you stay here any longer, it's all you're going to be wishing for," Jordan warns.

"Okay, I wish us all out of here!" Mal intones.

Thanks for dropping by. Don't let the lid hit ya on the way out.

WHERE DID MAL AND THE GANG GO?!

al, Evie, and Freddie enter the Auradon Prep dining hall. Freddie asks, "So I seriously have to take a class called 'Remedial Goodness?'"

Yup. There's a two-hour exam about smiling.

Smiling's super important in Auradon. Let's see what you got.

Jane's mom, Fairy Godmother, teaches Remedial Goodness, and is the principal of Auradon Prep.

Freddie tries to smile, but she looks sinister.

Evie tries to encourage her. "Try less teeth." Freddie makes an attempt to try less teeth.

"Better, but your eyes still look villainy," says Evie.

"Try smizing. It's smiling with your eyes. Apparently it's a thing good people do," adds Mal.

"Ooh, smells like lunch is ready," says Mal. The three walk over to the buffet tables laden with magnificent confections. Freddie examines the spread and gripes, until she dives for a plate of puffed pastry and shoves one into her mouth.

There is an ice sculpture shaped like Disney's Cinderella Castle on the buffet table.

Okay! Give me some of that puffed deliciousness!

Mmm . . . I wish I had more mouths.

Mal and the other VKs tried to steal Fairy Godmother's wand when they first arrived at Auradon Prep.

> Were we that bad when we first got here?

> Oh no, we were the picture of elegance.

Freddie continues shoving food into her face, until she bumps into Lonnie and drops a pie. "Get your own buffet table!" Freddie tells Lonnie, who leaves disgusted.

A mysterious hand reaches out from under the table and grabs the food from the floor.

> They say puffed deliciousness?

> I say puffed disastrous!

It's time for the annual Auradon Prep singing competition, and everyone is psyched to perform in the school auditorium. Lonnie, Audrey, Mal, and Evie are in the stage wings, all dressed up and ready to jam.

Ally was born in King George Town, Auradon— the former home of Cruella de Vil! She is Alice in Wonderland's daughter.

Hey, Ally. You okay?

"No! My partner lost her voice and can't sing tonight," Ally says. "I need to find a new partner now, or my chances of winning go down the rabbit hole!"

Just then Freddie approaches.

Alice arrived in Wonderland by falling down a rabbit hole.

You shrink one guy's head, and no one wants to sing with you.

Ally doesn't have a partner. Why don't you two sing together?

"A VK?!" Ally laughs, and turns to Freddie. "Are you magical? Do you sprout horns? Just how evil are you?" Ally turns to Mal and says, "I don't think I can sing with her. If I hit a wrong note, she might turn me into a frog!"

Never! I'd just shrink your head, like my last partner.

Oh, it's disgusting! But curious. Can I touch it?

Ew, can you guys talk about this somewhere else? We're up first.

Actually, we're up first.

"Sorry," Audrey sings, grabbing Lonnie. "Let's go."

Lonnie shrugs to Mal and Evie, and hurries onstage with Audrey to begin their performance.

Many famous bands tour Auradon, including Aladdin & the Lamps, The Sorcerer's Apprentices, The Dragon Slayers, and The Bad Apples.

Evie and Mal run after them and join Lonnie and Audrey in their song.

"Well, if it's a free for all, I might as well join in," Freddie says, dancing onto the stage.

"If Freddie can sing along, then so can I!" Ally says, running to join the others onstage.

The six girls perform a rousing, beautifully choreographed rendition of "Good Is the New Bad." The crowd goes wild, as everyone cheers and applauds.

Good IS the new bad!

10 SPIRIT DAY

It's Spirit Day at Auradon Prep! Jay, Carlos, Ben, and Audrey are hanging out in the stands on the tourney field. Across the stadium, Mal and Evie are walking over to them.

"I can't believe I let you talk me into doing this," Mal says to Evie.

Evie asks, "What happened to, 'Sure, best friend! Anything for you!'?"

"That was before I knew it would involve pom-poms," says Mal.

"Forget about the pom-poms, and focus on the super-awesome outfit we made," Evie says.

"It is pretty wicked, isn't it?" Mal agrees. "I think all cheerleading outfits should have spikes."

Tourney is the only sport played at Auradon Prep.

Wow! You look great. I'm so glad you're doing this.

You know me, anything to show my school spirit!

Jay is a star player on the tourney team.

Audrey turns to Evie and Mal, and hands them each a sheet of paper. "So, you guys know the cheer. 'F-I-G-H-T! What's that spell? FIGHT, FIGHT, FIGHT!'"

Evie asks, "Is it just me or—"

Mal cuts her off. "Does this cheer sound exactly like that spell my mom used to say to us when were kids? How did that go . . . "

B-I-T and E! What does that spell?

BITE, BITE, BITE!

Bark!

Mal and Evie continue the cheer together: "Speak no words, we'll cause a fright! What's a bark without a bite?!"

After this, everyone on the field starts barking like a dog!

Mal runs up to Carlos, who is sitting in the stands. "Bark! Bark! Bark!" she says to him.

"You accidentally turned everyone into dogs, and you want me to help you use your spell book to reverse it?" Carlos asks.

"But why don't you just spell them back?" asks Carlos. Mal growls at him. "Right . . . you can't because all you can do is bark!" Mal barks in agreement, but then Carlos notices Jay scratching himself on the field. He can't resist walking over to his friend.

Mal walks over and barks at Carlos. "Down girl! Heel!" orders Carlos. Mal begins to growl.

The spell is on page forty-three!

Carlos thumbs through the spell book. He reads aloud, "Bark! Woof! Bark! Bowwow! Bark! Grr!"

Mal repeats, "Bark! Woof! Bark! Bowwow! Bark! Grr!" When the spell turns the gang back into themselves, Jay glares at Carlos.

Carlos laughs nervously, and then an angry Jay chases him off the field.

E vie, Mal, Jordan, and Lonnie are talking
together in the science lab at Auradon Prep.
"Thank you so much for designing my
outfit for the hip-hop show," Lonnie says.

"Of course. Our pleasure," says Mal.

Then Lonnie says to Evie and Mal, "I just have
one question for you guys."

Lonnie is the daughter of Mulan.

Why are we making my dress in a science lab?

Great fashion is cutting edge.

"So, what's more cutting edge than creating
chemical compounds?" Evie asks.

Lonnie isn't sure.

"You guys said you wanted to look fierce,
right?" Mal reminds everyone.

"Super fierce," says Jordan.

"But also welcoming," says Lonnie.

Vibrant jewel tones with teal highlights make up Lonnie's signature style. The images on her skirt are origami cranes.

Mal shows them several sketches.

"You know what? I think we have just the thing," Mal says, and Evie holds up a beaker of phosphorescent neon liquid.

"Nuclear waste?" Lonnie guesses.

No! Well, not anymore.

This is going to make your dress glow in the dark.

Mal continues, "Dark . . . light. What is more fiercely friendly than that?"

Jordon says, "I love it."

"You want me to perform in the dark?" Lonnie asks.

With this stuff, you'll bring the house down . . . or burn it down. Just stay away from liquid nitrogen.

I can't hear you! I still can't hear you!

Later that night, Jordan steps onstage to warm up the crowd for the show. "What the what, Auradon? You ready for some awesome Lonnie hip-hop dancing extravaganza?" The crowd cheers.

Lonnie runs onto the stage as the crowd cheers her on. She begins to sing, "I'm Your Girl."

"Are we sure this is going to work?" Mal asks Evie.

Nope, but we like living on the edge.

Yes, we do.

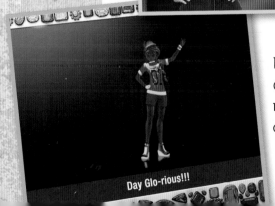

Day Glo-rious!!!

Onstage, Lonnie's neon hip-hop outfit glows in the dark, as she continues to rock her performance. The crowd goes wild.

12 MASH IT UP

Mal, Evie, Audrey, Freddie, Jane, Lonnie, and Ally are hanging out with Jordan in her lamp.

Jordan gets to the point.

> Okay, people, this is crunch time.

"Auradon Prep's annual Fighting Knight's ball is coming up, and we still don't have a theme for the party."

"Ooh, I know! Let's do a pretty, pretty princess theme," says Audrey.

"We did that last year, and the year before, and the year before," Ally reminds her.

Mal says. "I have an idea—"

Audrey cuts her off. "Let me guess! You want everyone to wear purple."

A full bow is Jane's signature icon.

"No!" Mal scoffs. But then she admits, "Yes."

What about a 'Who's the Fairest?' party?

Evie's signature icon is a cracked tiara.

"It'll be a competition. The winner will get everything and the loser will get nothing!"

Jane says, "That sounds mean."

Evie takes that as a compliment. "Thanks!"

How about a kick-boxing hip-hop ball?

"So, you dance while you punch your friends?" Jordan asks, sarcastically.

Freddie says, "Now, that's my kind of party."

Jane's mother turned a pumpkin into a carriage for Cinderella.

"Ooh! I love pumpkins," Lonnie says.

Audrey can't believe this idea. "You want to throw a garden vegetable party?"

The girls start talking over one another, tossing out ideas. Mal, Jane, Freddie, and Jordan use their magic to make their points.

> A Fighting Knights party!

> Magic Carpet party!

> A party in the dark!

> How about a wonderful Wonderland party?

> Neon Glow party!

Audrey's signature style combines dusty rose and and sky blue with gold accents. Her signature icon is a songbird in flight.

Freddie has an idea. "Why don't we just do all of our themes?" It'll be a mad princess, hip-hop, party in the dark, magic carpet, wicked, Wonderland, garden, neon lights party!"

"Wait!" Mal says. "A neon lights party! That's actually really cool . . . it could be some sort of neon light–filled mash-up of all our ideas . . . with everyone glowing via Evie's neon fashion invention!"

"Great!" Ally says. "I'll start working on the e-blasts."

"Just the right neon fashion will be . . . PHOSPHERESSENTIAL!!" says Lonnie, and everyone laughs.

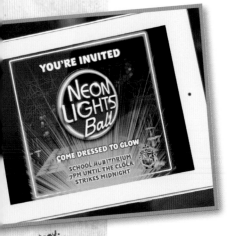

YOU'RE INVITED

Neon LIGHTS Ball

COME DRESSED TO GLOW

SCHOOL AUDITORIUM
7PM UNTIL THE CLOCK
STRIKES MIDNIGHT

M al, Audrey, and Freddie are hanging out in Audrey's room at Auradon Prep, while Audrey angrily brushes a rope of blonde hair.

All righty! Who's ready for party makeovers?!

Ugh, what does it matter? I wasn't even chosen as the QNLB!

"Is that a good thing? 'Cause that acronym doesn't sound good," says Mal.

"It's Queen of the Neon Lights Ball, duhzies!" Audrey says, dramatically. "And I. Did not. *Win.*"

"Oh, Freddie, did you just ask who did win?" Evie asks.

"No," Freddie replies.

"Oh, Mal, did you just ask where I'm going to put the crown?" Evie asks.

Mal says, "No."

"I don't know where. I'm running out of room for all of my crowns," says Evie. "Okay, Freddie, for your makeover, I'm thinking a little less voodoo, and a little more *new* do."

"No probs," Evie says. "Audrey, for your makeover, I'm thinking about some apple-red lipstick and some wicked Cheshire-cat eyes!"

"The only makeover I'm interested in is the one where I'm made-over from being the one who lost the crown, to the one who won," Audrey says.

"Oh, I forgot to bring that one, sorry!" Evie responds. "Mal, for your makeover, I want to see what you look like in purple."

Uh . . . I think we know the answer to that.

Purple tones make up Mal's signature style.

But Evie says, "That's not purple. It's aubergine."

"Hmm, I always thought of it more as eggplant," says Freddie.

"What is happening here?" Mal asks Audrey.

"I know, right?" Audrey responds. "It's clearly more of an amethyst."

Jane rushes in.

Guys, my mascot uniform is gone!

Why are you looking at me?

Because your bracelet was in my room. You must have dropped it when you stole my uniform!

Jane is the Auradon Fighting Knights tourney team mascot.

"I don't know why my bracelet was there, but I didn't take your uniform," Mal assures Jane.

"Maybe you spelled it away," suggests Audrey.

"What? Why would I do that?" Mal defends herself.

"Maybe you thought it wasn't fashion forward or something," Jane says.

That sounds like something I would do.

"Trust me," Mal says to Jane. "If I spelled away every single non–fashion forward item I saw every day, there'd be no clothes in Auradon."

Audrey asks, "So, you're saying you don't like the way we dress?!"

"No!" Mal insists. "What I'm saying is, I did not take the uniform. Seriously. I didn't do anything. Jane, I'm sure it will show up soon."

"I guess you're right," Jane says, hopefully.

"Yeah, this is Auradon. It's not like there's some thief in a cloak running around stealing things," Evie says. The girls all laugh at the thought.

The mascot uniform is a suit of armor.

Mascot uniform MIA!

lly has prepared a pre–Neon Lights Ball tea party for the gang in her shop. Mal, Evie, Jane, and Freddie are enjoying sandwiches. Jordan is looking around the shop. Ally appears from behind the store counter, wearing a gorgeous dress.

Ally loves to bake, serve tea, and host events! She is often found at her parents' teashop on the Auradon Prep campus.

Then Audrey rushes in.

"Is someone hurt?" asks Jane.
Audrey says, "No."
"Is someone really hurt?" Freddie asks, hopefully.
"No!" Audrey cries.

"Oh, is there an emergency?" Jordan asks.

Now the girls are alarmed.
Audrey starts to hyperventilate.
"It's okay," says Evie. "Everyone, just calm down." Evie holds up a dress.

Audrey tells her, "You know, for a VK look, it's actually pretty cute. I'm sold!" She runs out of the room and quickly returns, wearing the dress.

"Wow, how did you change so fast?" Evie wants to know. "It was like, right out of a cartoon."

No one notices that while Evie is talking, a hand reaches up from under the table, snatches the teapot, and replaces it with another teapot.

"My mom was raised by fairies," Audrey reminds everyone. "Quick outfit changes are a family skill."

Ally cuts in, "This deserves a celebration! Tea me, Mal!" But as Mal pours the tea, purple liquid gushes out of the pot and splatters all over Ally's white dress.

Audrey's mother, Sleeping Beauty, was raised by the three fairies, Flora, Fauna, and Merryweather.

"That's why you destroyed it," Ally reasons. "You're jealous. You VKs can't stand it if someone looks better than you."

Mal argues, "Ally, I swear, I didn't do this. But I can fix it . . . I think." Mal tries a spell, but orange splotches spread across the dress.

"Uh . . . okay, don't freak out!" Mal says. "Yet . . ." She tries another spell but rose-shaped splotches now emerge all over the dress. Mal gasps.

"Wait," says Freddie. "I actually really like it."

"You do?!" Ally asks. "You're just saying that!"

"No," Freddie says. "I mean it . . . it's really alternative."

"She means, it's very fashion forward," explains Evie. "If I didn't think I was already wearing the best dress, I'd be super jelly . . . but I do, so I'm not."

"You know what? I think it's cool, too!" Jane says.

"Really?" Ally asks.

"Really," says Jane. "Even the Queen of Hearts herself would be jealous of that number!"

"I would totally feature that on my Web show. 'VK gone viral!'" Jordan adds.

Again, no one notices, but the mysterious hand pops out from under the table and snatches a jar of sugar, replacing it with a new jar. . . .

Haute Dress or Hot Mess?

T he girls are still in Ally's shop, ready to go to the ball and waiting for their ride.

"Don't worry, guys, I'm sure Jay and Carlos will be here any minute," Mal tries to reassure everyone.

"You said that fifteen minutes ago," Ally says, impatiently.

I'm sure they are just around the corner.

How big is this carpet they're picking us up in?

Jay is a thief, but what he really steals is hearts.

Jordan answers, "It's a midsize, so we'll be fine. But from what I've heard about Jay, I'm sure it's stolen."

"Hey, Jay doesn't steal!" Mal says, defending her friend. But then she adds, "Much."

Jane is horrified. "We're going to be riding on a stolen carpet?!"

Freddie likes this. "All right! This party just got interesting."

"We need to figure out how to get to the party straightaway," Ally advises. "Jane, you're all magical now . . . can't you whip us up a ride?" Ally asks. Then she asks Jordan, "Do you have a spare magic carpet?"

Jordan is offended. "Oh, because I'm a genie who lives in a lamp I automatically fly around on an old rug?!"

"She didn't pass her carpet driver's test," Audrey whispers to Evie.

"I'm taking it again next week," Jordan says, defensively.

Thirteenth time's a charm!

I can help—

Ally cuts her off. "No offense, Mal, but the VKs are clearly not coming through today. Sorry."

Mal says, "It's all right."

"I mean, normally I would let you help out, but whenever you get involved it leads to disaster. No offense," Ally explains.

Mal is taken aback. "Okay . . . "

"It's because you destroy everything you touch. No offense," Ally continues.

"Do you know what 'no offense' means?" asks Mal. "'Cause I'm starting to take some."

Ally says, "No, no, no—please don't take it that way. It's that I don't trust you—sorry." Then she asks, "Jane, whaddya say . . . can you bibbidi-bobbidi us up some transpo?"

Audrey cuts her off. "No presh, but if I don't get to the party soon, I'm going to die."

"Jane, let's see what you've got," Jordan says.

Jane panics. "Uh . . . well, I'm really very new to this whole magic thing . . . " She looks out the window and says, "Bibbidi-bobbidi!"

A pumpkin appears in the middle of the road.

Fairy Godmother uses the phrase "Bibbidi-Bobbidi-Boo" when she casts spells.

"That's a vegetable," Freddie observes.

Jane corrects her. "Well, it's a gourd . . . "

"Gourd-geous, really!" Ally notes. "Does it fly?"

Jane objects, "It's not a flying pumpkin . . . "

"Oh," says Ally, "so we are heading to the party in some sort of pumpkin boat."

"It's not a boat!" exclaims Jane.

The girls keep guessing while Jane becomes ever more exasperated.

"Guys! Let Jane do her thing! Go ahead, Jane," says Mal.

"Thank you," Jane says, clearing her throat. "Like Cindy's pumpkin carriage, a legend to us all . . . an even sweeter ride shall take us to the Neon Lights Ball!"

POOF!

HONK!

Used french-fry oil can be transformed into a great alternative fuel known as biodiesel.

When an orange car appears, the girls congratulate Jane, who is just as surprised as they are to see the car.

"Sweet ride!" says Audrey. "Wait, this veggie car is carved right? I'm not going to get nasty, gooey seeds on my dress am I?"

"Nope," Jane confirms. "All clear. And it's green—runs on vegetable oil!"

As all the girls giggle and head out, Evie and Mal have a moment.

I can't believe Carlos and Jay flaked.

Evie agrees. "I know—and we've been working so hard to get people on our side."

"They better have a good excuse," Mal replies.

Mal's signature icon is a heart-shaped dual dragon.

If you ladies don't get in here, I'm going to turn into a pumpkin!

Jordan says, "That doesn't make sense."

"Your hair doesn't make sense!" Audrey says, as she gets into the car. But then she pops out and says, "No offense." Mal and Evie hop in, and the car peels away.

Unnoticed, the school mascot is hanging out in a tree before she jumps on a carpet and flies away. . . .

The VKs and AKs are all now rocking out at the Neon Lights Ball. Neon lights flash, while a spotlight shines on Ben and Evie.

"It's time for the crowning of the Neon Lights king and queen: Ben and Evie!" Ally announces, as she places outlandish crowns on Ben's and Evie's heads. Evie loves every minute, taking selfies and scrolling through her pictures.

I look so good. I don't even need a filter!

"The jewels on the crown totally match my eyes," Evie gasps.

Ben is not as in love with his crown, which keeps dropping and hitting him in the face, causing Mal to laugh. "I know I'm new to the whole crown thing, but I don't think plastic jewels are supposed to poke you in the eye," he says to her.

Staring at her pictures, Evie thinks Ben was talking to her. "I know. I really am."

Then Ally announces, "And we now invite our king and queen to do a solo dance!"

"Dance for me," Evie says to Mal, taking off her crown and gazing at it lovingly. "I've got a date with some bling." Then she says to the crown, "Oh, crowny, I love you," and walks off with it.

Evie's most cherished possession is a shard of her mother's magic mirror.

"But you've gotta admit, they make a lovely couple." Mal and Ben watch as Evie waltzes with her crown.

"They do," Ben agrees. "But I can't let crowny out-dance me." He offers Mal his arm. "Shall we?"

"We shall . . . and stuff," Mal says, as Ben escorts her onto the dance floor. The spotlight finds them and they get ready for their solo dance. But when the music doesn't start, they look around, awkwardly.

Where is the music?

Maybe it's a really slow, slow dance?

"Uh . . . excuse us!" Ally announces, and then in a loud whisper she asks, "Lonnie, what's going on?!"

Lonnie is alarmed. "I don't know what's happening! Nothing's working!" she gasps.

Lonnie was born in Northern Wei, Auradon. Her signature icon is a cherry blossom branch.

Someone cut the DJ cord!

Ally addresses the crowd. "Sorry! We're having some technical difficulties. Please hold." She rushes over to Ben and Mal, and says, "Someone cut the DJ cord!"

"What?" asks Mal. "Who would do that?"

Freddie walks over and says, "Don't worry."

I will sing for you.

"I insist . . . I got this . . . seriously. I've got it all under control. Go on, dance!" After Freddie sings a few bars with just her guitar, Lonnie hooks up an MP3 player to some speakers, creating a full-blown version of the song.

Ben and Mal reluctantly dance a slow dance, as Freddie continues to sing, in spite of the AKs giving her weird looks. Students are averting eye contact with her. She doesn't get it.

"Hmm . . . from what I see, it looks like Freddie has kinda saved the party. I don't know why you guys are throwing her shade," says Jordan.

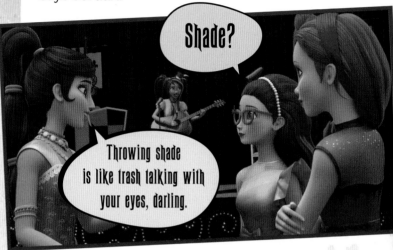

Shade?

Throwing shade is like trash talking with your eyes, darling.

"Like this," Jordan explains. She throws Jane some serious shade.

"I know what it means," Jane says, defensively. "I just wanted to see if you did."

Jordan throws her shade again.

Audrey says, "It's just kind of strange that right after the DJ cord was cut she jumped in, all ready to sing."

"Maybe she wanted to help!" Jordan argues.

"Or maybe she wanted the spotlight," Jane says.

"I bet she cut the DJ cord!" says Audrey.

Jordan warns, "You better stop trash-talking before you cut a vocal cord!"

"Hey, whose side are you on, anyway?" asks Audrey.

Jordan responds, "The side that writes songs that good! I smell something viral! Go on, girl!"

As the song comes to an end, Freddie notices people throwing her shade. She looks at Lonnie and gives her a thumbs-up, before exiting the stage.

Lonnie transitions the music into Ben's coronation party song, and everyone comes out onto the dance floor to dance.

But behind the DJ booth, one gloved hand holds a cut stereo cord, while another gloved hand holds a sword. . . .

Carlos's signature style mixes red with black and white.

J ay and Carlos rush into the Neon Lights Ball, looking disheveled.

"Hey, thanks for picking us up three hours ago," says Mal.

"But we didn't pick you up," says Jay.

Mal says, "I was being sarcastic."

"I didn't get that," says Jay. "Living in Auradon is really messing with me."

Audrey, Jordan, and Ally head over to the group. "Where were you guys?" asks Jordan.

"We got carpet jacked!" Jay exclaims.

Jordon can't believe this. "What? That doesn't happen in Auradon."

"Apparently, it does," says Carlos.

"So who did it?" Evie demands.

"Dunno," says Carlos. "We were getting ready to head out, and the rug was pulled from underneath our feet! Literally!"

Jordan asks, "So you never saw who did it?"

But Jay is distracted by someone walking into the dance. "Hey, isn't that the mascot?"

Ally says, "Oh, good—Jane found it."

"Found what?"

The gang turns around to see Jane, who is not wearing the mascot outfit.

"Jane!" Mal says.

"You're not in the mascot uniform," observes Evie.

"Uh . . . yeah," Jane says, "'cause this is a formal night. And besides, how could I be in the mascot uniform? It was stolen, remember?"

Ally is confused. "But if you're not in it, then who is . . ."

Everyone starts to panic. The lights go out. Everyone screams. Ben is heard, struggling. When the lights come back on, Ben is gone.

Periwinkle, powder blue, and fuscia make up Jane's signature style.

Everybody begins to search frantically for Ben. When Mal runs toward a table, the gang follows.

"Oh! We need search music," says Lonnie.

"Ben?" Mal says, checking underneath the table. Not finding him, Mal pops her head above one of the flower decorations, and everyone follows suit.

Audrey says, "I don't understand. How can Ben just disappear?" She turns to Mal.

Moments after meeting CJ at the Neon Lights Ball, the gang is still in shock.

"Wait a minute . . . ," Mal says. "All the bad things that have been happening around here . . . it was all you."

"Oh, stop. You'll make a girl blush," CJ says, flattered. "Actually, I'm kinda offended that you didn't figure it out sooner."

"Where's Ben, CJ?" Mal wants to know.

"Wave hi, Benny!" CJ says.

Ben struggles to wave. "So, Mallsy, what's first? Storm the castle? Take prisoners? Manically laugh in people's faces?"

Mal runs to untie Ben. "Ben, are you okay? Here, let me help you." Then she asks CJ, "Why would you do this?"

"Well, why wouldn't I?" CJ replies. "We're villain kids, it's what we do!" Then she turns to Jane.

You really should lock your stuff away . . .

4

Evie says, "Why would you even ask that?"

"Well, Ben did magically disappear and Mal does have magic," Ally points out.

SO . . .

"So what?" Mal demands.

Ally says, "So you could have done this."

"Maybe it's part of your plot," Jordan guesses.

"My plot?!" cries Mal.

"You know, to take over Auradon and stuff," Ally accuses.

Mal replies, "And why would I do that?"

"Because you're a VK?" Audrey reasons.

As the girls continue to fight, someone swoops down on a rope.

"CJ!" exclaims Mal.

"Hey, Mallsy. Miss me?" CJ greets Mal, winking at her. "Oh, I was going to give up dramatic entrances. So flashy. But what can I say . . . "

I'M HOOKED!

CJ laughs, making a hook symbol with her finger. "Get it, Mal-icious?!"

"Let me get this straight," Jordan says to Mal. "You guys know each other?"

Evie explains. "CJ is Captain Hook's daughter."

Ally says, "Well, that does explain the seaweed stench."

"That's rotting kelp," CJ says, proudly.

"Great. Another VK," comments Audrey.

"Stealing that mascot uniform was like taking candy from a baby," CJ tells Jane.

"And Mal," CJ continues, "framing you with that bracelet was just icing on the old cake."

Then CJ says to Audrey and Ally, "I tried ruining your party dresses, but it seems these two VKs have gone soft." She points to Evie and Mal. "They just had to . . . what is it you Auradon kids call it? 'Save the day?' Oh, and let's not forget the no-shows," she says, looking at Carlos and Jay. "I got to hand it to little miss bibbidi-bobbidi over here . . . a pumpkin car? Not my thing, but you pulled it off."

"Stealing the carpet from you two was probably the most fun I had yet!" CJ tells Jay and Carlos.

You stole the carpet? Nice!

"You know," says Jay, "maybe we can meet up after your hostile takeover. You can give me some pointers."

But CJ says, "Quiet, I'm soliloquizing." She turns to Freddie. "And then, the grandest of them all . . . cutting that DJ cord, so our little Freddie could have her moment in the spotlight. It was the least I could do, as a thank you for sneaking me into Auradon."

Mal continues to untie Ben and turns to Freddie. "Freddie?!"

Surprise?

Freddie says, "I can explain—"

CJ cuts her off. "So can I. She was following orders. Freddie is my second in command."

Uh . . . no . . . we're partners!

CJ says, "Exactly. I tell you what to do, and you do it. Partners."

"Excuse me?" Freddie asks. "I spent my whole life living in my dad's shadow. I'm not going to live in yours, too."

CJ takes this in. "I get it. My dad never let me steer the ship, either. But we don't have to be like our parents."

"Exactly," Mal agrees. "We make our own choices."

"We can veer starboard on the squall together," says CJ.

"Um . . . translation?" demands Freddie.

Partners.
For realz.

"What?" asks Mal.

"We're going to pillage and plunder together!" says CJ.

I thought we
were friends.

Freddie insists, "We are friends."

"Then why are you pillaging and plundering me?" asks Mal. "Okay, that just sounds weird."

CJ explains, "Because her captain commands her to pillage and plunder."

"Can we go back to you 'commanding' me?" Freddie asks CJ. "That's not very partnerly. I know the AKs are lame—"

Audrey cuts her off. "Excuse me?!"

Freddie continues, "But at least they don't go back on their word."

"You're saying that like it's a bad thing," says CJ.

"Because it is!" Jane exclaims.

Mal shakes her head.

"I'm disappointed in you, Freddie," says CJ. "I thought you were badder than this—"

Do you forgive me? Are we still friends?

"Looks like I'll have to be partnerless in crime," CJ continues. "So long, *squarest* of them all!" And with that, CJ grabs a rope and swings out of the window and out of the party.

"Sorry about that," Freddie apologizes to Mal. "I guess for being kinda lame, Auradon is kinda cool."

Mal considers this, looking around at everyone. Evie nods, and Mal says, "If I didn't forgive every friend with a conniving stowaway, I wouldn't have any friends."

Jane asks, "Shouldn't we go after her?"

"I dunno," answers Mal. "Freddie? Are there any other surprises we need to know about?"

"Not from me," Freddie responds.

Mal says, "Well then, we can go after her later. . . . "

"But she committed a crime—" Jane points out.

Mal cuts her off. "The bigger crime is wasting this awesome Neon Lights Ball. And I think we may know a little bit about crime, right Evie?"

Evie agrees. "Right!"

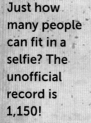

Just how many people can fit in a selfie? The unofficial record is 1,150!